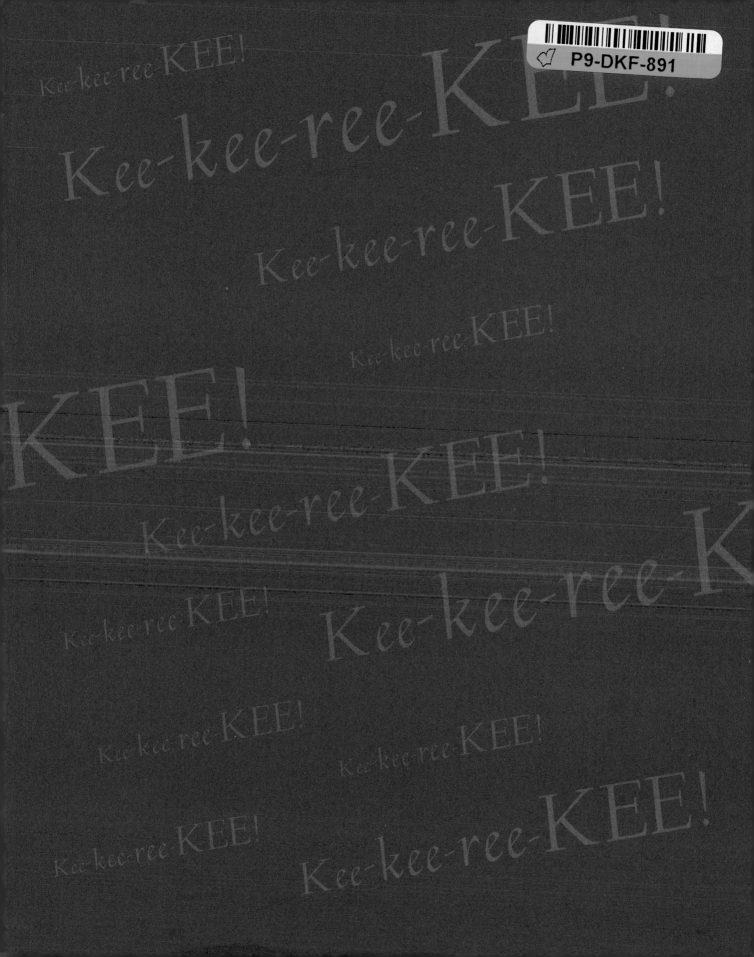

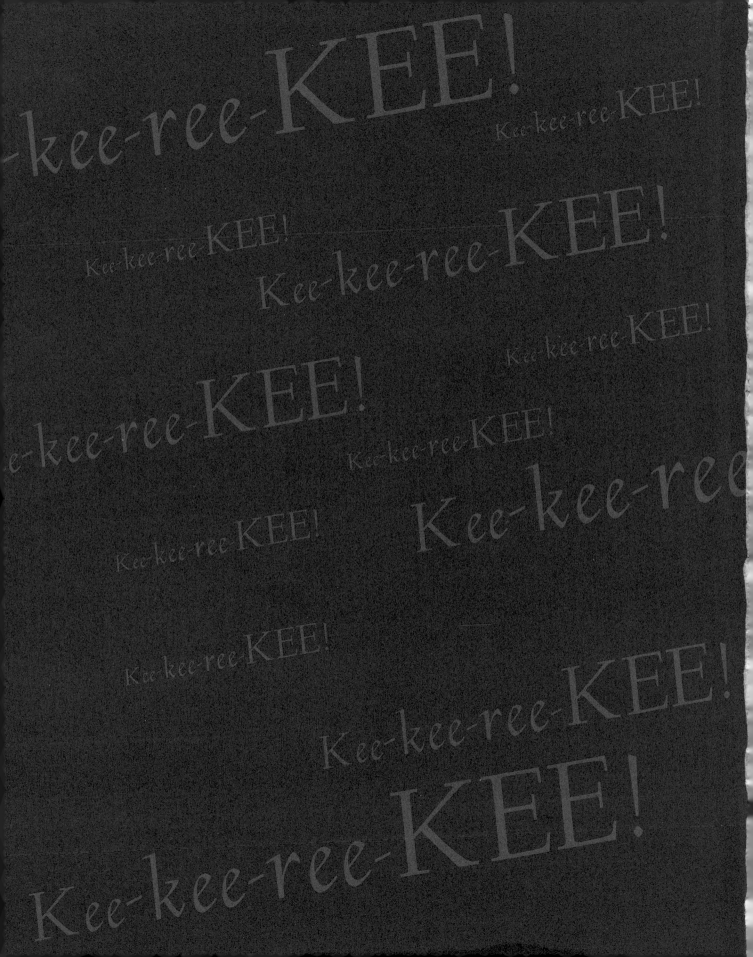

The Rooster Who Would Not Be Quiet!

BY CARMEN AGRA DEEDY

ILLUSTRATED BY EUGENE YELCHIN

SCHOLASTIC PRESS • NEW YORK

Library of Congress Cataloging-in-Publication Data

Names: Deedy, Carmen Agra. | Yelchin, Eugene, illustrator.
Title: The rooster who would not be quiet! / by Carmen Agra Deedy ; illustrated by Eugene Yelchin.
Description: First edition. | New York : Scholastic Press, 2017. | Summary: "The mayor of the noisy village of La Paz
instituties new laws forbidding all singing, but a brave little rooster decides he must sing, despite the progressively
severe punishments he receives for continuing to crow. The silenced populace, invigorated by the rooster's bravery,
ousts the tyrannical mayor and returns their city to its free and clamorous state."—Provided by publisher.
Identifiers: LCCN 2016013458 | ISBN 9780545722889 (hardcover : alk. paper)
Subjects: | CYAC: Villages—Fiction. | Noise—Fiction. | Singing—Fiction. | Roosters—Fiction.
Classification: LCC PZ7.D3587 Ro 2017 | DDC [E]—dc23
LC record available at http://lccn.loc.gov/2016013458
10 9 8 7 6 5 4 3 2 1   17 18 19 20 21

Printed in China 62   First edition, February 2017

The display was set in Amigo Std Regular.
The text was set in Depdeene H.
Eugene Yelchin's artwork was rendered in
oil pastel, colored pencil, gouache, and acrylic.
Book design by Marijka Kostiw

To Ruby, Sam, and Grace.

And to real roosters everywhere.

—C.D.

For Isaac and Ezra

—E.Y.

Once there was a village

where the streets

rang with song

from morning

till night.

Dogs bayed,
mothers crooned,
engines hummed,
fountains warbled,
and everybody sang in the shower.

Everyone and everything had a song to sing.
This made the village of La Paz a very noisy place.
It was hard to hear.
It was hard to sleep.
It was hard to think.
And *no one* knew what to do.

So they fired the mayor.

Now they were a very noisy village . . .
without a mayor.

So they held an election.

Only Don Pepe promised peace and quiet.

He won by a landslide.

The next day, a very polite law appeared
in the village square:

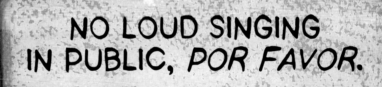

**NO LOUD SINGING
IN PUBLIC, *POR FAVOR.***

Things were getting better already.

But more laws soon followed:

NO LOUD SINGING AT HOME.

NO LOUD SINGING AT ~~HOME~~.

NO ~~LOUD~~ SINGING ~~AT HOME~~.

¡BASTA! QUIET, ALREADY!

Until finally . . .

The noisy
village
of La Paz
was silent
as a tomb.

Even the teakettles
were afraid to whistle.

Some people left the village — singing loudly.
Others stayed behind and learned to hum.
The rest were just grateful to have a good
night's sleep, for crying out loud.

Seven very quiet years passed. Then one evening,
a saucy *gallito* and his family wandered into the village
and roosted in a fragrant mango tree.

When the little rooster awoke the next
morning, he did what roosters were born to do.

He sang:

Kee-kee-ree-KEE!

As his rotten luck would have it, the mango tree grew beneath the cranky mayor's window.

Uh-oh.

"You, there!" groused Don Pepe. "No singing!
It's the law!"

"Well that's a silly law," said the merry *gallito*.
"Smell this sweet mango tree! How can I keep from
singing?"

"Humph! Then I'll chop down that stinky tree!"
huffed Don Pepe. "Will you sing then?"

The plucky *gallito* shrugged. "I may sing a less
cheerful song. But I will sing."

And he did.

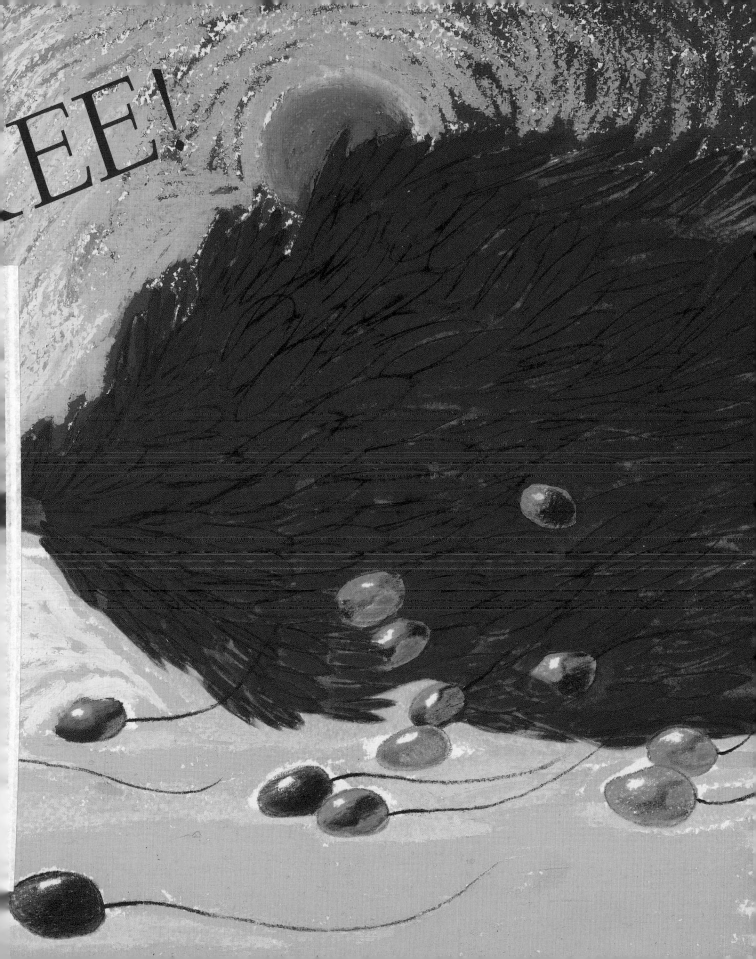

"Still singing?" snapped Don Pepe. "You have no tree. Remember?"

"I have no tree," said the *gallito*. "But I have my hen and chicks. How can I keep from singing?"

"Will you sing if I throw you in a cage — alone?" threatened Don Pepe.

"I may sing a lonelier song," said the stubborn *gallito*. "But I will sing."

And he did.

Kee-k

ee-ree-KEE!

"Why are you singing now?" growled Don Pepe. "You have no hen and chicks."

"No hen and chicks." The *gallito* sighed. "But I still have corn to eat. How can I keep from singing?"

"And if you have no more corn?" asked the mayor.

"I may sing a hungrier song," said the headstrong *gallito*. "But I will sing."

And he did.

Kee-kee-ree-KEE!

"Aren't you hungry, you crazy bird?" wailed Don Pepe.

"*Claro*, of course," said the *gallito*. "But if the sun can still shine despite this world's troubles — how can I keep from singing?"

"And if you NEVER see the sun again?" snarled the mayor. And he ran for a blanket to cover the rooster's cage.

"I may sing a darker song," the brave *gallito* called after him. "But. I. Will. Sing."

And he did.

Kee-kee-r

As the *gallito's* song echoed down the soundless streets
of La Paz, it stirred an old familiar longing for a time when
everyone and everything had a song to sing.

Kee-kee-ree-KEE!

Kee-kee-ree-KEE!

Kee-kee-ree-KEE!

Kee-kee-ree-KEE!

Kee-kee-ree-KEE!

Kee-kee-ree-KEE!

Kee-kee-ree-KEE!

Not so with Don Pepe.
Singing gave him indigestion.

The next day, Don Pepe stumbled
out to the yard in his nightshirt. He tore
away the blanket and pleaded:
"You have no tree to roost in,
no hen and chicks to comfort you,
no grain to fill your belly,
no sun to drive away the shadows.
WHY oh why are you still singing?
Promise to stop *and I will set you free!*"

One by one, a quiet crowd began to gather in Don Pepe's yard.

"I sing for those who dare not sing — or have forgotten how," said the *gallito*. "If I must sing for them as well, señor, how can I keep from singing?"

"And if I have you made into a soup?" the mayor thundered. "I suppose you will still sing if you are DEAD?"

The entire village held its breath
waiting for the *gallito's* reply.

"Dead roosters sing no songs,"
he said.

"HA!" crowed Don Pepe,
sure he had won.

"But a song is louder than one noisy little rooster and stronger than one bully of a mayor," said the *gallito*. "And it will never die — so long as there is someone to sing it."

And there was.

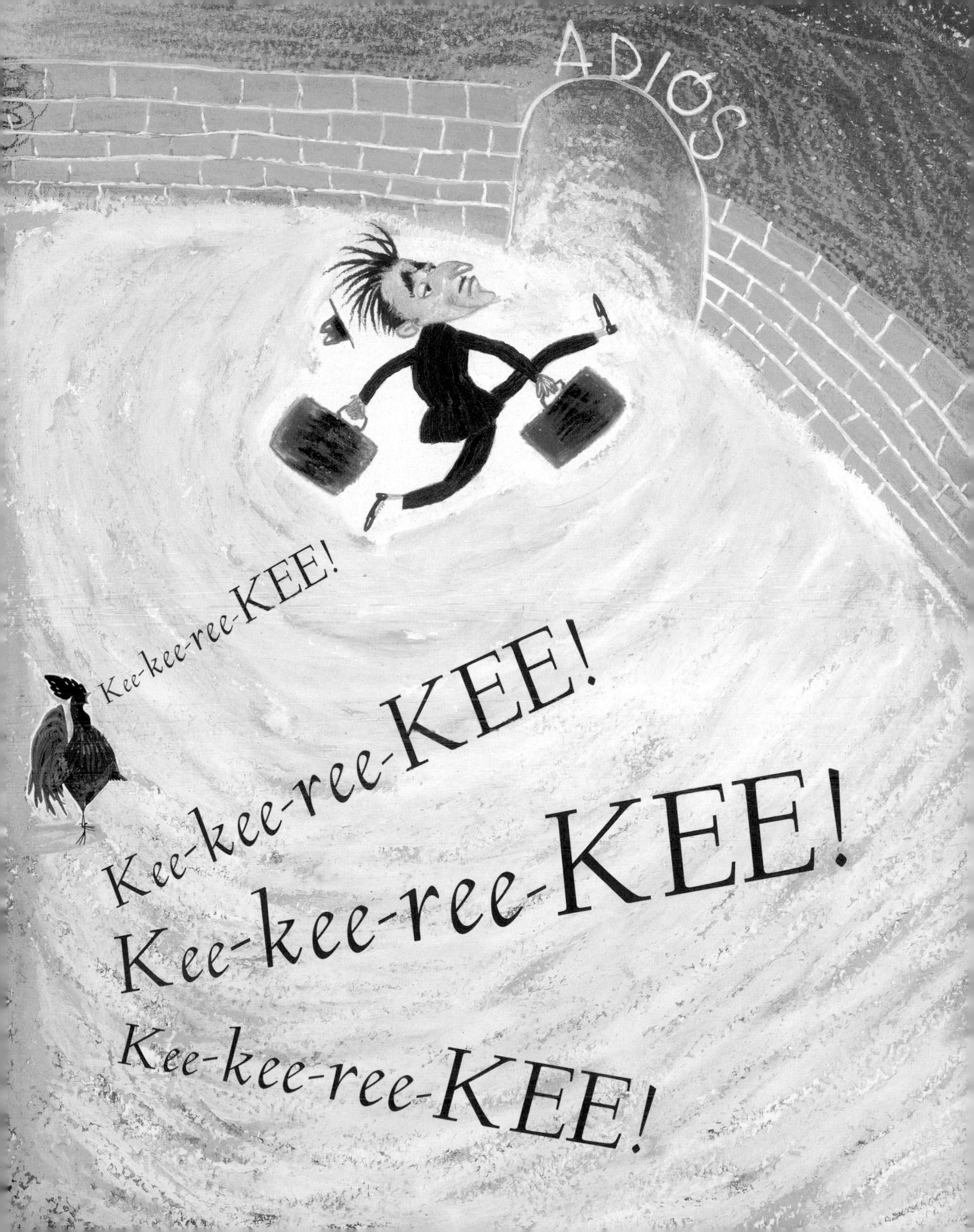

Once again there was a village where the streets rang with song from morning till night.

This made for a very noisy place to live. And that's just the way everyone liked it.

AUTHOR'S NOTE

Roosters sing at sunrise; they also sing
at noon, sundown, and in the middle of night.
Roosters sing when they please, and that's all there is to that.

Much like roosters, human children are born with voices
strong and true — and irrepressible.

Then, bit by bit, most of us learn to temper our opinions,
censor our beliefs, and quiet our voices.

But not all of us.

There are always those who resist being silenced,
who will crow out their truth,
without regard to consequence.

Foolhardy or wise, they are the ones
who give us the courage to sing.

—Carmen Agra Deedy

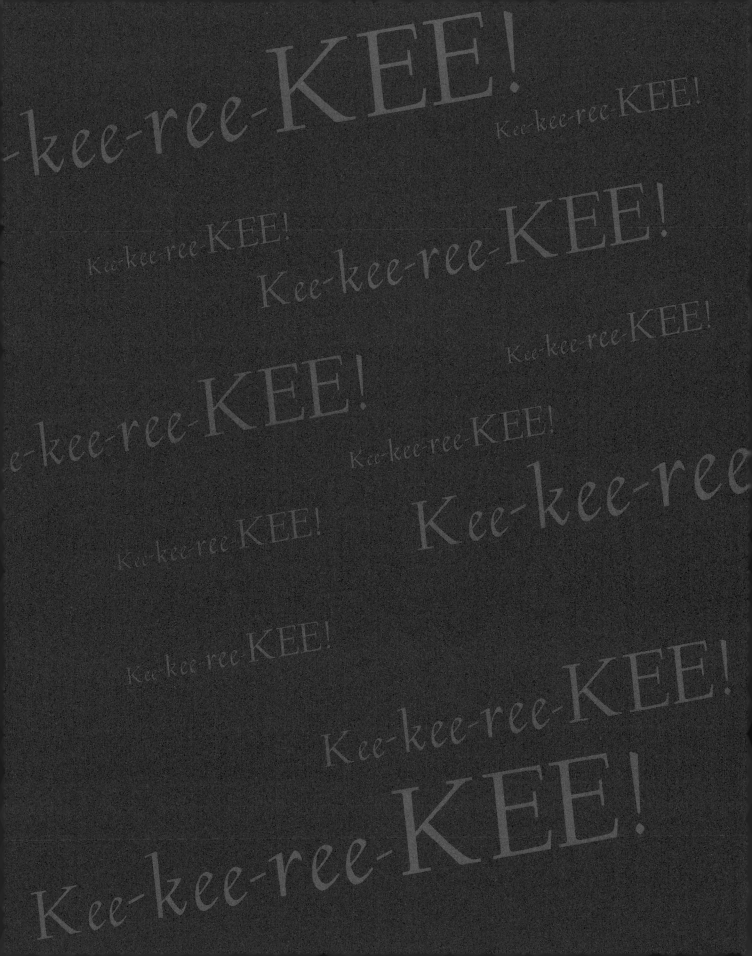